Making
Music

The Silver Balloon
Edwina Victorious
Above and Beyond

Making Music

Susan Bonners

FARRAR STRAUS GIROUX
NEW YORK

Library of Congress Cataloging-in-Publication Data
Bonners, Susan.
    Making music / Susan Bonners.
        p.   cm.
    Summary: When Annie, her mother, and baby brother move to a new
home, they have a lot of work to do, but Annie finds joy at the house of a
neighbor who plays piano.
    ISBN 0-374-34732-8
    [1. Music—Fiction.   2. Piano—Fiction.   3. Single-parent families—Fiction.
4. Moving, Household—Fiction.   5. Neighbors—Fiction.]   I. Title.

PZ7.B64253 Mak 2002
[Fic]—dc21

                                                                    2002021611

To John Zmudka
and to all the people who created that magical,
now rare, sound—piano music floating through a
screen door on a summer night

Contents

Making
Music

Moving Day

ANNIE STOOD ON THE BACK PORCH of the new house, holding her baby brother, Tommy, by the hand. Through the screen door they watched the moving van drive away. For the last half hour, Tommy had hardly made a sound, just stared in astonishment as two men had pounded up the steps carrying in their furniture and boxes containing everything they owned. Now the house was quiet.

Annie helped Tommy over the doorstep into the kitchen. Her mother turned on the faucet. Rusty water ran out.

"That's sediment in the pipes," she said. "It will go away in no time."

She tried to open the window above the sink, but it was stuck.

Tommy started to cry. Annie's mother picked him up and rocked him as tears rolled down his fat cheeks.

"Oh, dear. He probably wants his bear. When the movers came, I threw it into the last open box. I thought I'd remember which one, but I don't. It's got to be here somewhere."

They pulled open box after box. Mixing bowls, pots, and ovenproof dishes soon covered the table and countertops. No bear appeared. Tommy sat in a corner, whimpering and banging a pot lid on the floor.

"All this and still no plates," said Annie's mother, shaking her head.

They ate lunch over newspapers.

"It's like a picnic," her mother said in a cheery voice, but Annie could tell she was tired. Some of the hair had come loose from her braid. Once in a while, she rubbed her forehead.

Annie was thinking hard. She'd watched the moving man carry the last box to the van . . .

"Now I remember!" She ran to the living room and started shoving boxes around until she found the one marked "Linen Closet." She yanked off the tape and pushed aside the flaps.

"Here it is!"

She plopped the bear in front of Tommy. He squealed and pounced on it, burying his face in the fur.

"Oh, Annie, thank you," her mother said, hugging

her. "See how happy he is now! Would you go to his room and look for his sheets and blankets? I'll keep going in here."

Annie started up the stairs, then went into the living room instead. She squeezed between the boxes to reach the piano. The other people had left it behind when they moved. On the music rack was a book with a faded torn cover, *Forty Big Hit Songs to Play and Sing.*

Annie pushed back the keyboard cover and quietly pressed a few keys. She thought about how her mother's younger brother, Johnny, would sit with her on his lap while he played the piano, her hands on top of his. He had started to teach her how to play. But they didn't live near Uncle Johnny anymore. Now they were a three-hour drive away.

She opened the music book. The pages seemed to be written in a secret language. If only she could read it, she could make music, too, music that would make people feel happy if they were sad or lonely.

She covered the keyboard and went upstairs.

In the middle bedroom, the boxes were stacked against one wall. Red stickers on all sides identified each one as Tommy's.

The stickers had been her mother's idea. She liked to organize things. Blue stickers for Annie, yellow for herself, red for Tommy, green for everything else.

Annie began pulling the packing tape off the boxes. Besides the bedding, she decided to get out all of Tommy's favorite toys. That would make the afternoon go a lot easier.

Annie had lined up Tommy's alligator, his dolphin, his koala, and his giraffe when her mother called from the bottom of the stairs.

"Annie, we got a mail delivery."

Her mother was in the living room, shuffling through a handful of envelopes. "I didn't think we'd get anything so soon. This looks like a card from Aunt Helen . . . this is some junk mail . . . here's a postcard from my friend Barbara . . . and here's a letter for you and Tommy from your dad." She handed it to Annie.

Annie opened it and read it quickly all the way through, then again more slowly.

"The university got more money for the dig he's on, so he'll be in Greece for two more months. He says congratulations on the new house and to please send him some pictures of it and pictures of us, too."

Even when he wasn't in some foreign country, Annie's father didn't live with them anymore, not since her parents had separated and her father had gone back to school to get a degree in archaeology. That had happened before Tommy was born. Annie was still trying to get used to the three of them being on their own.

By dinnertime, they had found the plates. One or two kitchen boxes hadn't turned up, so they used custard cups for glasses and dishrags for napkins. Annie thought it was sort of fun to have things topsy-turvy, but Tommy didn't like it at all. He fussed as his mother pinned a towel around his neck.

"You miss your blue elephant bib, don't you, sweetheart? Blue elephant is hiding just now. He'll come out tomorrow."

When dinner was over, Annie opened a box marked "Back Porch." Her roller skates were on top.

"Why don't you go out and skate until it gets dark?" said her mother. "Just on this block."

The skates made a pleasant whirring sound as Annie pushed off down the front sidewalk. Barely staying on her feet, she managed the turn onto the broad sidewalk. Skating had never been easy for Annie, but she was determined to learn. The sky darkened from blue to purple-gray as she worked her way from one end of the block to the other, dodging the cracks and broken places.

Annie was ready to quit for the evening when she heard piano music. It was coming from the house with the birdbath in the yard, two doors down from her house. Someone must have turned on a radio. A lively dance tune floated through the screen door.

She found herself skating in time to the beat. *Tum-ta-ta-ta. Tum-ta-ta-ta.* The music steadied her. She stopped thinking about her feet. She passed her house and kept going to the end of the block. The sound grew very faint, then louder as she came back. As she glided past the birdbath, Annie realized that she wasn't hearing a radio. Someone was playing a real piano. She slowed down and stepped onto the grass. She tried to see into the living room, but the window was too high.

"Annie! Time to come in!"

She'd have to go. As she skated home, she imagined her own fingers racing up and down the keyboard.

"Good night, pumpkin," said her mother as she kissed Annie. "Tomorrow we'll start really fixing up this place." She switched off the light and closed the door.

Annie lay in the dark wide awake. Boxes crowded her bed. She imagined she was on a raft, floating in the sea with all of her things bobbing in the water around her.

For the first time since Tommy was born, she had her own room. Annie and her mother had talked about the fun she was going to have decorating it—no more baby wallpaper or decals.

From the bedroom at the end of the hall, she could hear boxes being opened. Her mother was unpacking. Annie wished she would go to bed. She needed to rest. Ever since she'd told Annie—back in March—that they'd have to move because of the new job she was taking, she'd often seemed worried and anxious.

Annie had trouble picturing what a radio producer did, even though her mother had explained it to her. What she could see was that, since March, the telephone rang off the hook and her mother sat at her desk filling out papers. Summer would be over, and they'd hardly had time to ride bicycles or watch scary movies together.

Annie pulled the covers up around her. She missed Tommy's soft, steady breathing. Morning seemed a long time away.

Lost

ANNIE WOKE UP to the chittering of squirrels in the tree outside her window. She pulled on her clothes, splashed water on her face, and went downstairs. Her mother was in the living room trying to squeeze glue out of a plastic bottle.

"This must have been left open. I thought I'd try to fix the wallpaper where it's peeling."

Lots of things were peeling in their house, like the paint on the bathroom ceiling. Their new house was really an old house. Where paint had chipped off the kitchen doorframe, Annie could see at least five different colors. She heard thumping when she turned on the hot water, and the door to the bathroom didn't shut right.

Her mother sighed. "I can do this after breakfast." She brightened. "I found the toaster. And Tommy's bib."

Annie picked dandelions from the backyard and put them in a pickle jar to decorate the table.

"I wish I knew where my address book got to," said Annie's mother as she set a bowl of cereal in front of Tommy. "I want to phone Aunt Helen and thank her for the card. But one thing I've got to do this morning is find the houseplants before they all die."

Annie was washing the breakfast dishes when she heard her mother call from the living room.

"Found 'em! Oh, dear. Two of the pots broke," she said as she held up the African violets. "I'm almost sure I saw some flowerpots on the workbench in the basement. Annie, would you get them for me? Be careful on the stairs. The light down there doesn't work for some reason."

Annie hadn't been to the basement. She didn't like basements. Their old house hadn't had one. She didn't like the idea of going by herself, but she was anxious to help.

The door to the basement was next to the pantry. At first, the door seemed stuck. Then Annie noticed the old-fashioned key in the lock. She turned it and opened the door onto a flight of wood plank steps. As she started down, the air became sour and damp. A weak ray of sun slanted through one small, grimy window. In the gloom, Annie could make out cement tubs, a washing machine, and a set of shelves.

A dark shape perched on the edge of the lowest shelf. When Annie went closer, she saw it was a pair of ice skates, the black leather cracked and the blades rusted. An open box of dust-covered marbles had been left next to the skates.

In the far corner of the basement sat the furnace, like a giant squid with six huge tentacles that reached up through the ceiling. Annie knew they were the pipes that carried hot air upstairs when the furnace was working, but they looked like powerful grasping arms. Across the sleeping monster's fat middle was an iron door like a square mouth.

The flowerpots were on the workbench. Annie picked one up. Inside the pot, her fingertips brushed something soft and sticky—a web. With a shudder, she flung the pot away. It rolled in a half-circle, just missing the edge. A long-legged spider slipped out of the hole in the bottom and skittered across the bench.

Annie felt like bolting up the stairs, but she'd feel silly telling her mother that she was afraid of a little spider. She thought of all the things she'd learned on nature programs about how interesting spiders were and how beneficial to the environment. It was no good. They still frightened her.

The spider disappeared into a crevice in the concrete wall.

Annie looked around. A curtain rod was leaning against the shelves. Using the rod, she slowly turned the dropped flowerpot in all directions. No more spiders there. She pushed over another one with the rod and rolled it around in the same way. No spiders there, either. She set the rod against the wall, grabbed the flowerpots, and ran upstairs.

"I thought you got lost down there," said her mother. "I was going to send a search party."

"I was just looking at some stuff I found," Annie said. "Here're your flowerpots."

"We have to get some groceries," her mother said as she tapped the plants into their new pots. "The stores aren't far."

They put Tommy into the stroller and started off.

"Watch how we go," said Annie's mother, as they headed for the main street, "so you'll learn the neighborhood."

Annie began counting blocks—two to the main street, then they turned right. They began to pass apartment buildings on the same blocks with houses.

Three boys on bicycles streaked past them, yelling and laughing. Annie wondered if they'd be in her grade when school started. In her old neighborhood, she would have known them, at least by sight. She would have known if they were okay or not.

A paper cup skipped down the street as the wind picked up. Sheets of newspaper slid by. Gum wrappers and bits of foil began to litter the sidewalk, more with every block. The streets where they'd lived before weren't like this. No scrap of paper there ever stayed on anybody's lawn for more than a day. Even the busy streets were swept clean.

When they got to the stores, Annie didn't see one that looked familiar. No big white Finnigan's Supermarket, no Bob's Franks-To-Go, not even a Make 'Em Fresh Donuts. And where were the parking lots?

The stores here were tiny and jammed together. Annie's mother maneuvered Tommy's stroller around crates of fruit and racks of dresses put right out on the sidewalk.

They passed a grocery with open double doors. The white-aproned workers and most of the customers looked like the people in *Our Asian Neighbors*, the book Annie's third-grade class had read last spring. They clustered around the counter, talking in a foreign language. Annie looked at the vegetables on display. She didn't recognize a single one.

"That looks like the place." Her mother pointed to a store across the street. When they went inside,

Annie was relieved to see shelves full of familiar foods.

She had a hard time steering their shopping cart down the narrow aisles without hitting anybody else's. Her mother had to keep asking clerks where things were, but at last they had all the items on her list.

While Annie and her mother piled groceries onto the conveyer belt at the checkout, the lady at the register was chatting with a dark-haired man ahead of them.

"Buenos días," said Annie's mother as she moved forward.

The lady smiled broadly. *"Buenos días!"* She pointed to Annie. *"Es ella tu hija?"*

"Sí. Somos nuevos en esta ciudad." Annie's mother laughed. "I hope I just said, 'We're new in this city.' My high school Spanish is pretty rusty."

The lady looked at Annie again. *"Tu niña es muy bonita."*

Annie smiled to be polite, but she had no idea what the lady had said, and she didn't like being left out of the conversation.

"What did she say?" Annie whispered as they went out through the automatic door.

"She asked if you were my daughter, and then she said you were very pretty."

"Oh."

The wind had picked up while they were in the grocery, and the sky had darkened.

"I guess they were right about that forecast for rain," said Annie's mother.

They hurried down the block toward home. Storekeepers were opening awnings and pulling in racks of clothing. The first drops of rain hit when they turned off the busy street. As they went up the back steps, the drizzle turned into a downpour.

"That was close," Annie's mother said when they got inside. She went to the front hall. A manila envelope had gotten stuck in the mail slot. She tore it open.

"This is health insurance stuff from my new job. I'm supposed to fill out these forms and return them right away."

More papers for her mother to worry about.

"Annie, after lunch, while I'm doing this paperwork, I want you to unpack your clothes. Your dresser is in place and I put hangers in the closet."

That sounded like a really boring job, but Annie couldn't think of any way out of it.

A half hour later, she was hauling the first box over to her dresser. She opened it, dug out an armload of sweaters, and tossed them into a drawer.

She was on the fourth box when her mother

leaned in the doorway. "Good job, sweetheart. I've got to lie down for a couple of minutes. Tommy's asleep in his crib." She went to her room at the other end of the hall.

Unpacking when everybody else was asleep was even more boring, especially on a dreary afternoon like this one. Annie went to the window to see if the rain had stopped.

While she was there, someone in a hooded yellow slicker walking a big black dog stopped at the tree in front of their house. Annie guessed that the dog walker was a girl, but she couldn't tell for sure because of the hood. She hoped it was a girl, someone she could be friends with. She'd make friends at school, but that was more than a month away.

Without looking up, the person walked on with the dog.

Annie had a better idea than hanging up clothes. She'd unpack her horses and set them up on her shelf unit, just the way she'd had them in her old room.

They were the first things she'd packed weeks ago. The job had taken a whole afternoon and filled two boxes. Each horse was cushioned in a cocoon of tissue paper so the plastic wouldn't get scratched. The stable had had to be fitted in, along with sections of pasture fencing.

She'd made sure to put blue stickers on the boxes. Then, with a marker pen, she'd drawn on her brand— two interlocking five-point stars. On one star, the three lines that formed an "A" were made thicker than the others.

One of the marked boxes was under a pile of blankets. Annie shoved them aside and opened the box. As she freed each horse from its tissue, she laid it on the bed. The blaze-faced mare, her foal, the pinto pony, and the palomino were soon joined by the Arabian stallion, the quarter horse, and the Morgan. Two more foals, the Thoroughbred, and the Clydesdale lay on the bottom, along with some fencing and parts of a stall.

Some of Annie's favorites were yet to come, in the second box: the Appaloosa, the chestnut mare, and the blood bay stallion that she'd named Red River. Uncle Johnny had given her that one. Some of the other ones were presents, too, but the rest she'd paid for out of her allowance.

She picked up all the tissue paper and stuffed it into the empty box. Then she turned to the cluster of sealed boxes. Only five of them were left. The double-star brand wasn't on any of them.

Annie shoved the boxes around. She checked all the sides twice, but she could see the double star wasn't there. Her stomach felt queasy. All the boxes with blue stickers were supposed to be in her room.

One must have gotten mixed up. That would be easy. More than a dozen boxes were stacked against the living room wall. Boxes filled the space under the dining room table and surrounded the piano. Tommy's things had all been unpacked. Annie wasn't sure about her mother's.

She tiptoed to the room at the end of the hall. On the bed, her mother was sound asleep. Every box had been emptied and flattened.

Annie went to the living room. She pushed and pulled boxes to see the hidden ones. Green stickers. She looked under the dining room table. More green stickers.

Now Annie's stomach was completely upset. She wanted to tell her mother what had happened. Her mother would know what to do. She always did. When things went wrong, she never yelled or cried. She figured out something to do. But her mother needed to sleep.

Annie sat down on the footstool to think. What could have happened to the box? Then she remembered. Her mother had told her that three or four families had their furniture on that van. Maybe the box had gotten mixed up with somebody else's stuff and delivered to their house. But how could Annie find out who they were and where they lived?

The moving company would know. Her mother could call the moving company when she woke up. Annie looked at the kitchen clock. Four-thirty.

If the box was delivered to somebody else, maybe they'd keep it, or lose it, or throw it out. Right now, they could be putting it out on the sidewalk with the trash.

Annie went to the pile of papers on the kitchen counter and paged through them. Halfway down, she found a piece of paper with the name of the moving company and a phone number.

Annie thought for a minute, then dialed the number. A lady answered. She sounded older than Annie's mother.

"Sanford Brothers Moving and Storage. May I help you?"

"My name is Annie Howard and you moved my mother and me yesterday. We're missing a box. Maybe it got delivered to the wrong people."

"It's probably not missing, dear." Even though the lady's voice was polite, Annie could tell she thought she was talking to a dumb kid. "Your mother probably hasn't unpacked it yet."

"We're sure it's missing. My mother's unpacked

everything." Annie thought that stretching the truth would be okay. It would take forever to explain about her mother's sticker system.

"Well, your mother can submit a claim form for the value of the contents. Have her call me."

That meant Annie would never get her horses back.

"My mother wants the box. Can you ask the other people who had their stuff on the van?"

"It would be better if your mother would file a claim." The lady began to sound impatient. "Sometimes people just put things in the attic and don't look at them for years."

That was the scariest idea yet. Attics got hot as ovens in the summer, maybe even hot enough to melt plastic.

"This box has a special mark. It would be easy to find." Annie heard her voice starting to shake, but she was determined not to cry. "All my horses are in there. I've been collecting them for years. I saved up to buy them and one of them was a special present. The other people might throw them out. They wouldn't do that if you called them."

When the lady spoke again, her voice wasn't impatient anymore.

"I'm sorry. I didn't understand. I'll make some

phone calls for you—Annie, is it? And I can get in touch with the driver." Annie heard some papers being shuffled. "You know, I was crazy about horses, too, when I was young. Now, what did you say your last name was?"

Annie gave the lady the information she needed.

"I'll get right on this. We'll track down those mustangs and lasso 'em for you."

"Thanks!" Annie hung up feeling much better, even though she was still worried.

For a few minutes, she fiddled with a pencil on the message pad, hoping the phone would ring. Then she realized that Tommy was cooing to himself. She went to his room. He was standing in his crib. Annie saw that he'd been able to reach the container of cornstarch on his changing table. Now he was squeezing the upended plastic bottle with both hands, watching with great interest as cornstarch poured onto his mattress.

Annie rushed to the crib and clapped her hand over the holes in the bottle. She was trying to wrestle it away from him when the phone rang. She heard her mother pick up the extension on her night table and answer in a sleepy voice. Annie couldn't make out what her mother was saying, but she didn't dare let go of the cornstarch. She had just gotten ahold of it when her mother came to the doorway.

"That was a Mrs. Boquist from the movers. She said you'd called her. Something about a missing box. What's going on?"

Then she saw the cornstarch. She pulled Tommy out of the crib. "I never fall asleep like that in the afternoon. I guess I was up too late last night. Annie, take him while I strip the bedding."

After the sheets had been shaken out, Annie bundled them into the hamper and followed her mother and Tommy to the kitchen. While water was coming to a boil in the kettle, Annie explained about phoning the movers.

"That was good thinking, Annie." Her mother reached into the cabinet for a tea bag. "That box is somewhere. It didn't just disappear. That call from Mrs. Boquist was to let us know that she tried to contact the driver, but he's probably getting dinner now. The people who got their delivery ahead of us haven't been home, but she left them a message." She patted Annie's shoulder. "I think they'll find it."

Annie wasn't so sure.

When she went out to skate that evening, the rain had stopped. The sidewalk puddles had all dried up.

Here and there, rays of sun lit up tree branches. Annie wobbled down the front sidewalk, stretching out her arms for balance.

The piano music was playing again. This time it wasn't bouncy. It was smooth, like a gently rippling stream. Annie imagined she was a leaf floating on the current. Her arms relaxed. She began to feel that maybe everything would be all right.

On the fifth trip down the block, the music changed to a march, the notes crisp and sharp. Annie pushed off strongly on the beats. *Tum ta. Tum ta.* Then the music changed again. Annie speeded up her skating in time with it.

A distant voice called, "Becky, Becky!"

Somebody by that name must live nearby.

"Becky!"

Suddenly, behind her, Annie heard panting and a dog's running feet. She glanced over her shoulder. The big black dog she had seen from her window was coming after her. Annie tried to slow down. The dog might stop chasing her if she slowed down.

Her hands were out for balance. The dog could grab one in his jaws. He was right behind her. She tried to veer away from him and fell.

The big black dog began licking her hand.

"Rebecca! Shame on you!" A girl rushed up to Annie. "Did she knock you down? Are you okay?"

Annie's hands still stung from the fall. She brushed them together to get rid of the sidewalk grit.

"I'm okay. She didn't knock me down. I just fell."

Her tail wagging, the dog began eagerly licking Annie's face.

"Rebecca, that's enough," said the girl, pulling the dog away. "She got out our gate. It was supposed to be closed. Sorry." She helped Annie to her feet. "I'm Karen. I haven't seen you around before."

Now that Annie was standing next to her, she realized that Karen was probably a seventh or an eighth grader.

"I'm Annie. We just moved in."

"Oh, your house must be the green one at the end of the block. I noticed that the 'For Sale' sign was gone."

"That's us," said Annie.

Karen clipped a leash to Rebecca's collar. The three of them headed back to Annie's house. The music had stopped.

"I won't let Becky get out again."

"That's okay," Annie said, rolling up to her front steps. "We're friends now."

New Neighbors

THE NEXT MORNING, while her mother put up curtain rods, Annie sat on the lowest front step, rocking Tommy in his stroller. In time with the rocking, she sang one of the songs Uncle Johnny had taught her.

"From this valley they say you are going.
  We shall miss your bright eyes and sweet smile,
  For they say you are taking the sunshine
  That brightened our pathways awhile."

Of all the songs she'd learned from Uncle Johnny, she liked that one the best. Whenever she got to the part about "leaving the valley," Annie pictured someone getting on a train while a cluster of sad-faced people waved goodbye.

She looked two houses down. She hadn't seen anybody go in or out. Whoever lived there loved to garden. The yard was filled with flowers. A flock of sparrows fluttered and preened in the birdbath. Suddenly they scattered.

A gray-haired woman came from the far side of the house. She looked as if she might be dressed up to go somewhere. Annie's mother didn't wear stockings unless she was going to work or to someplace special. In one gloved hand, the woman carried a pair of clippers. She studied a rose, then snipped it off and set it in the basket on her arm.

Annie grabbed the handle of Tommy's stroller and ran with it to the rosebush where the woman stood looking over another blossom.

"Hello," said Annie. "We just moved into the green house over there. I'm Annie. This is my baby brother, Tommy. Are you the person who plays the piano?"

The woman looked around. She seemed surprised to see Annie.

"Why, yes, I am. I guess you heard me playing."

"I wish I could play the piano. I'll bet you took lots of lessons."

"Yes, I did," said the woman, smiling. "Oh. I'm Mrs. Bergstrom. I'm pleased to meet you both."

Mrs. Bergstrom looked elegant. She wore pearl earrings and a watch with tiny diamonds on it.

"We have a piano," Annie said. "Some of the keys don't work, but it has a music book with it. Did you know the people who used to live in our house?"

"I'm afraid not, Annie. I don't know many people in the neighborhood anymore. Most of the people I knew have moved away. I'm sure the new people are very nice, but they're mostly younger than I am."

"I wonder if your piano is the same kind as ours. I could tell if I saw it."

Mrs. Bergstrom put another rose in her basket. She smiled. "I guess you'd like to see my piano."

"Oh, yes!" Then Annie remembered. "Can I take Tommy? I'm supposed to watch him."

"Oh, dear!" said Mrs. Bergstrom, looking down.

Tommy was tugging on some lily stems, trying to stuff the flowers into his mouth. Annie pried open his fist. When he screamed, she handed him a plastic ring. "It's okay. I'll hold him."

Mrs. Bergstrom looked worried. "We'll have to watch him."

When she walked in the front door with Tommy in her arms, Annie saw why Mrs. Bergstrom was worried. The sofa and chairs were velvet. Figurines filled the shelves. Pinpoints of sun sparkled in the chandelier over the dining room table. On an end table stood a framed photograph of a man in a suit.

"Do you live here all by yourself?"

"Yes. That was my husband. He died a few years ago."

The piano stood in the middle of the living room. It was black and as shiny as a mirror. Annie wondered if Mrs. Bergstrom polished it every day.

"It's a grand piano." Mrs. Bergstrom lifted the entire top of the piano and propped it up with a stick. They all looked inside. "Isn't it beautiful?" She seemed to be looking at it for the first time. "It's like a harp lying on its side. Watch the hammers while I play."

Her fingers danced lightly over the keys. Annie shook her head.

"I could never play as well as you, not if I practiced my whole life."

"Nonsense. Of course you could. You just need a good teacher. Now, I was a very good teacher."

"You were? Could you teach me?"

Mrs. Bergstrom stopped playing. "Well, I haven't taught for many years. I'm retired, Annie."

"But you could teach if you wanted to."

"Teaching is tiring. I'm too old for it."

Annie nodded to hide her disappointment. Mrs. Bergstrom probably knew everything about music. Tommy squirmed in her arms and reached for the stick that was holding up the piano top. "I guess we'd better go now. Thank you for showing me the piano."

"You're welcome, Annie. I enjoyed it. I just realized, I haven't had visitors from the neighborhood for a long time."

When Annie got home, she described the grand piano to her mother.

"I'm afraid ours isn't what you'd call grand," her mother said, "but at least we can get it tuned one of these days. By the way, I phoned Cathy this morning. She'd love for us to stop by this afternoon."

Her mother's friend lived a few blocks away. When her mother started her new job in September, Annie would spend her after-school time there.

At lunch, Annie fiddled with her tuna salad sandwich. She was not looking forward to this visit. She did not want to stay with this person she didn't know. She wanted to go to a place like the day care center arranged for Tommy. He'd have playmates. But that was only for preschoolers.

After lunch, the three of them started off for the main street. This time, they turned left. They passed block after block of houses so close to the sidewalk Annie could almost reach in the front windows.

Then they crossed a four-lane street and everything changed. This block was a row of mansions like giant gingerbread houses. One was like a castle. Lots of them had peeling paint. That puzzled Annie.

"Do rich people live here?" she asked.

"Rich people used to live here," her mother said. "Now these places are all broken up into apartments. People like us live here."

Annie didn't want to live here. These grand places weren't friendly at all. They peered down coldly from the top of steep hills. Iron fences made the yards look like cemeteries.

Annie wondered if she'd dreamed about a place like this. The last house on the block, all spires and turrets, was so familiar. Then she remembered. It was just like the one on the cover of her book—*The Haunted House of Beacon Street*. Except that the house on Beacon Street wasn't painted pink. Annie thought that the color was very odd.

Her mother squinted up at it.

"Four forty-three," she said. "We're here."

Oh, no, thought Annie. Not this creepy place.

With Tommy on her mother's hip and Annie lugging the stroller, they navigated the long flight of crumbling steps to the porch. Annie counted eight doorbells. Her mother pushed the one labeled "Michaels."

They waited. Crows squabbling on the roof made

a terrible noise. Suddenly the door swung open. In the dim hallway stood a tall woman with dark bushy hair and dangling earrings. She sprang forward and threw her arms around Annie's mother.

"Jay-Jay! Welcome to the Pink Palace!"

She ruffled Tommy's hair. "How're you doin', dollface?" He gurgled happily.

The woman turned to Annie. "Hi, I'm Cathy. Wow, are you ever the picture of your mother."

Annie didn't know what to say, but she didn't have to answer. Cathy slipped her hands around Tommy and hoisted him onto her shoulder.

"Onward and upward," she said.

As they entered the hallway, a jumble of impressions rushed at Annie—faded wallpaper, threadbare carpet, a dusty mirror.

"Take a deep breath," Cathy said. "It's the fourth floor."

As they trooped up the creaking stairs, Annie was surprised to see that her mother's friend wasn't wearing shoes. Her bright yellow blouse looked like silk.

On the top floor, Cathy held open a door. "My own small bit of Shangri-la," she announced with a sweeping gesture.

They walked into a sunlit room. Plants cascaded

from hanging pots. The fringed rug looked like a magic carpet.

Then Annie saw the fish tank. It was enormous. She had no idea people could have tanks that big in their houses.

Cathy and her mother began a stream of talk, but Annie went straight to the tank. She was fascinated to see that some of the fish had whiskers. Huge snails scoured the glass with their rasping tongues while iridescent fish created a kaleidoscope of colors.

Cathy stooped down next to her. "Like my aquarium, Annie? There's a shark in there. See if you can find him."

"There is?" Annie was particularly interested in sharks. She had written about them for her science project last May. Her mother and Cathy retreated to the bedroom to change Tommy's diaper, but Annie remained watching the tank intently.

A minute went by, then two, then five. No shark. Cathy was teasing her. How could a shark be in there? He'd eat all the other fish. Annie felt stupid.

She listened to the women in the other room laughing and talking. Cathy kept calling her mother "Jay-Jay."

Annie was annoyed. She had never heard her

mother called "Jay-Jay" before. Why should anybody call her mother by a special nickname that nobody else used?

And she couldn't remember when her mother had been in such a happy mood. For months, Annie had been doing her best to help and not give her mother more things to worry about. Now her mother was happy because she was with this person that Annie had never even met before. It wasn't fair.

They came out of the bedroom. Cathy flopped into an armchair. Suddenly she jumped up again.

"I'm babbling on and this poor kid is probably starving." She disappeared into the kitchen and returned with a platter heaped with oatmeal cookies—Annie's favorite. "A little bird told me you liked these, so I made some this morning."

Annie took one, a very small one. "Thank you," she said in a polite voice. Cathy scooped up a handful of cookies and plopped them on the coffee table. "Have a bunch."

Annie took a tiny bite. It was a terrific oatmeal cookie. Somehow, that was annoying, too.

While Tommy crawled around mouthing a cookie and grinding crumbs into the rug, Annie's mother and Cathy laughed about their school days together and adventures they'd had. Annie's mother had never told her these stories.

Cathy talked about moving into her apartment the year before and how she'd gone back to school to learn jewelry making. She showed them the work table she had set up in the kitchen and the tools she used to form her materials.

"This is my newest design." She held up a necklace made of a line of leaping cats. Annie had never seen one like it.

"You'll be able to watch Cathy work when you stay with her after school," said Annie's mother as they all sat down in the living room again.

Annie wanted to see that. But she couldn't figure out how she felt about this woman who swooped around like a great bird and knew all kinds of things about Annie's mother that Annie didn't know. And she liked to tease people, which was mean.

Tommy yawned. Annie's mother stood up. "We've got to go, Cathy. He's overdue for a nap."

"Not without these." Cathy began dropping cookies into a bag. "By the way, Annie," she said, handing her the bag, "did you find my shark?"

Annie shook her head.

"Come." Cathy knelt down in front of the tank.

"There he is." She pointed. On the gravel bottom, a slender fish rested against a rock. It was marked with black and white bands from nose to tail fin. Annie guessed it was six inches long.

"He's a banded cat shark," Cathy said.

This couldn't be a shark. Annie remembered her report.

"A shark has to keep moving to breathe. He's not moving."

"Hey, you know something about sharks," Cathy said. "You're right, most sharks do. But this is a perching shark. He doesn't have to move. Except when he wants to."

"Why doesn't he eat your fish?"

"He doesn't eat live food. Cat sharks are scavengers. I feed him cut-up fish that I buy in the supermarket."

"How come he's so small?"

"He's a baby. He only hatched a month ago. I'll keep him until he's a couple of inches longer. Then I'm going to give him to a friend of mine who has a bigger tank."

Annie wondered how big that could be.

Just then, the fish moved away from the rock. Annie could clearly see the shape of the fins and the body. It was a shark, a beautiful miniature shark.

Annie was sorry she'd thought Cathy wasn't telling the truth—and very glad she hadn't said anything about it.

Tommy yawned again.

"I hate to break up the party," Annie's mother said, "but we'll be back soon."

Cathy came down the stairs with them, carrying the stroller. At the door, she gave Annie's shoulder a squeeze and hugged her mother and Tommy again. "So long, guys."

"I wasn't sure you were having a good time at Cathy's, except for seeing the shark," Annie's mother said at dinner. "You were very quiet until then. Was something bothering you?"

"No." Annie picked at her green beans. "Why does she call you 'Jay-Jay?' "

"Oh, that was Uncle Johnny's name for me when he was a baby, before he could say 'Jane.' I told Cathy about it and she started calling me that."

"Did Uncle Johnny ever meet her?"

"Oh, yes. She came to our house a lot."

"Does he like her?"

"Yes, I'm sure he does."

"I guess you really like her. You were talking a mile a minute."

"Well, because we lived in different places we haven't seen each other for many years. We just phoned each other and wrote letters. Annie, I'm sure something's on your mind. Can you tell me what it is?"

But Annie couldn't. When she tried to think of an answer, everything swirled around in her head— the fish tank and the cat necklace and Uncle Johnny. Then Tommy started pounding his table.

"May I be excused, please? I'll miss the music."

"Okay. Don't skate after it's dark. If you want to listen until the music's over, sit on our steps. We can talk later."

But they didn't talk later. The music went on that night until Tommy was in bed. When Annie came in, the phone rang. Aunt Sharon was on the line. Annie blew a good-night kiss to her mother. Aunt Sharon liked to talk.

Locked Out

"THIS MORNING'S JOB," announced Annie's mother at breakfast the next day, "is clearing away the stuff that's blocking the outside door to the basement."

Annie could think of things she'd rather do with her morning—like visit Mrs. Bergstrom—but she didn't mention them.

When the dishes were done, Annie's mother carried Tommy outside and settled him in his stroller at the foot of the wooden steps to the back porch. Then she and Annie went down the cement steps under the porch.

The "stuff" turned out to be a tangle of rakes, shovels, hedge clippers, and a wheelbarrow, all wedged in front of the basement door. The key to the puzzle was moving a cement column about two feet high. They wrestled with it.

"I guess we'll have to use the inside door to get

back and forth to the basement for now, Annie. We can't lift this thing."

"What is it?"

"I think it's the bottom of a birdbath."

"Can we put it out?" Annie thought of Mrs. Bergstrom's yard and the birds splashing like happy toddlers in a wading pool.

"I don't see the top."

"There it is!" A large cement dish was partly buried in the gravel under the back porch.

"Annie, it's cracked. It won't hold water."

"Let's try. Please."

They tried. They set the dish on the grass and filled it with water. Twenty minutes later, Annie watched the sun dry up the last spots of moisture around the crack. Not even a simple birdbath worked around this place.

Annie's mother saw how disappointed she was. "Maybe we can buy a new one when we get the house set up," she said as she strung a clothesline across the yard.

With all the things that needed to be fixed, that would be never.

After lunch, Tommy fell asleep on the living room floor. With Annie to watch him, her mother brought up a load of laundry from the basement and went out to hang it.

Annie's job was to unpack books and sort them according to subject. Building the tidy stacks made a pleasing order. Annie was almost at the bottom of the third box when she put her hand on a thin, spiral-bound book—the missing address book. She checked to see that Tommy was asleep. Then she grabbed the book and ran through the kitchen and back porch, out the screen door, and down the steps.

Bedsheets flapped in the wind. The backyard was like the deck of a ship under full sail. Annie didn't see her mother. Maybe she was in the basement by the washing machine.

Annie climbed into the wheelbarrow in the basement stairwell and peered through the door. After the blaze of white sheets, this place was the sunless sea floor. The giant squid slept in its corner. Her mother wasn't there.

Puzzled, Annie climbed out of the stairwell again. She stooped down and scanned the lawn below the sheets. Across the yard, she saw a pair of sandaled feet.

"I found your book!" Annie ran through the maze of billowing cloth. Her mother looked around in surprise.

"Annie, where's Tommy? He can't be left alone."

"He's asleep, I looked." She held up the book. "See?"

"Yes, but—"

Her mother was interrupted by the sound of a door slamming.

Annie turned with a start. Through a porch window, she saw that the door to the kitchen was shut.

Annie pounded up the steps just ahead of her mother. She flung the screen door open and made a lunge for the knob of the kitchen door. Locked. On the other side of the door, Tommy giggled.

"Turn the latch back the other way, Tommy!" called Annie's mother.

Tommy giggled again. Annie knew that giggle. Tommy was playing his favorite game—hide-and-seek. Annie felt a pang in the pit of her stomach. She should never have left him, not even for a second. They heard a scraping noise.

Annie's mother looked through the door.

"Tommy's pulling a chair out. Tommy—no climbing!"

She turned to Annie. "I hooked open the basement window above the workbench to air the place out. Stay with Tommy. I'll get in."

While her mother ran around to the side of the house, Annie watched helplessly as Tommy pulled himself up on a chair, then struggled to get a knee onto the tabletop.

"Tommy, let's do 'Itsy Bitsy Spider,' okay? 'Itsy bitsy spider crawled up the water spout . . .'"

Hearing the familiar song, Tommy stopped climbing. He touched his fingers to his thumbs to imitate a spider the way Annie had taught him.

Annie thought of the spider in the flowerpot. She hoped there weren't any more. Her poor mother.

"Annie." Her mother appeared at the bottom of the steps. Her hands and shirt were streaked with dirt. "You'll have to do it. I can't fit through the window."

I'm a little teapot, short and stout . . .

As she crawled backward on her stomach through the open window, Annie tried to keep her mind on the song her mother was singing to Tommy.

Here is my handle, here is my spout . . .

She inchwormed her legs through the window, then hugged the windowsill as she began lowering herself.

When I get all steamed up, then I shout . . .

The toes of her sandals scraped down the inside wall.

Tip me over and pour me out!

Her right toe touched the workbench. She eased her hold on the windowsill and dropped the rest of the way.

"Annie, are you okay?" her mother called.

"I'm okay!"

She hopped off the workbench and bounded up the plank steps. Without a light, she felt for the doorknob, twisted it, and threw all her weight against the door. It didn't give. She was locked in the basement.

Annie felt something brush her face. She slapped both cheeks and shook her head violently. She wanted to kick down the stupid door.

The sound of cabinets being opened came from the kitchen. How could babies get into so much trouble so fast? Why couldn't he just sit still for two minutes at a time?

It was her fault. She was supposed to watch him. Now he'd climb on something and fall, or break a glass and cut himself. They'd have to call an ambulance.

"Tommy," she called, "let's do the teapot again the way I showed you." As Annie sang, she constantly rubbed her cheeks and forehead, sure that some crawly thing was trying to land on her face in the dark.

Tommy, who was tired of being a little teapot, began rattling the kitchen stool.

Annie felt her way down the steps and circled the basement. She didn't know what she was looking for, maybe some kind of tool. But no tools had been left, only rusty skates and marbles—somebody else's junk—in this horrible smelly cave. She had to get out of this place and find another way into the house.

The window above the workbench was too high to climb out now that she was inside. She turned the latch on the door to the outside and pushed it open as far as she could—about an inch—before it hit the wheelbarrow. Above her on the porch, her mother called down.

"Annie! Can't you get in?"

"The door's locked up there," Annie shouted back.

"Annie, I'm sorry. I forgot. I locked it myself when I came up with the laundry so Tommy wouldn't fall down the stairs. Try to keep him by that door. I'll have to run to a neighbor's and phone the police. Wait a sec—that's it, Tommy. Turn that. Turn that key, sweetheart!"

At the top of the wooden steps, Annie heard a metallic click. A shaft of light appeared as the door to the kitchen swung open. Tommy was silhouetted in the doorway. Cooing his questioning sound, he toddled forward. Annie bolted up the steps and grabbed him.

She caught a glimpse of her mother's frantic expression through the kitchen door before she got to the latch and let her in.

"Annie, I was so scared," her mother whispered, hugging her and Tommy together. Then she looked at Annie and burst out laughing. "You look like a coal miner!"

Annie put Tommy down and ran upstairs to the bathroom mirror. Her face was covered with black smudges.

"I'm sorry for laughing." Her mother stood in the bathroom doorway with Tommy in her arms. "I'm just so relieved. You were very brave to climb through that window. It's not your fault the door was locked.

And I should have had my keys with me. I'll have to put a higher latch on the door to the basement."

Annie shoved her washcloth around the soap dish and scrubbed it hard across her face. It wasn't funny. Being stuck in a dark basement with things crawling on you wasn't funny at all.

Annie was rinsing off the soap when the phone rang. Her mother went to answer it. Annie shut off the water to listen.

"Yes . . . yes . . . oh. Okay. Thanks for calling, Mrs. Boquist. I'll tell Annie."

Her mother reappeared in the bathroom doorway. "Mrs. Boquist left another message for the people who got the first delivery off the van. She did talk to the driver. He doesn't remember any boxes like the ones you described, but he has two more loads to deliver. He's got three hundred miles to go for the first one, so we'll have to be patient."

"Couldn't he look in the van now?"

"From what Mrs. Boquist said, he's on the road. He won't be stopping until sometime tonight."

At dinner, Annie's mother told her again how brave she was to climb into the basement, and how Tommy would have fallen down the basement stairs if she hadn't been there. She didn't even mention that it was Annie's fault for leaving Tommy alone, which was nice of her. But Annie felt worn out. Her favorite T-shirt would probably never get clean. Her horses were being carted all over the country. And she was still irritated about the visit to Cathy's.

The only good thing that day was the music in the evening. Annie didn't skate long. After a few minutes, she came back to the front steps to sit and listen. Upstairs, Tommy was squealing and splashing his bathwater, but Annie was following the patterns the music made in her head.

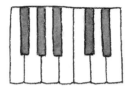

Broken Chords

THE NEXT MORNING, Annie finished sorting the last of the books and putting them on the shelves. The space around the piano was cleared. She pushed back the keyboard cover and started to play her favorite song.

From this valley they say you are going.
We shall miss—

That was all she could play. She started over and over, but the rest wouldn't come. She could hear the melody in her head, but the piano notes were gone, the left-hand part Uncle Johnny had taught her that sounded like a guitar being strummed. If only she could read notes, Uncle Johnny could send them to her in a letter. She could practice until she knew the song by heart. Then she would play it for Mrs. Bergstrom.

Annie helped her mother wash windows and hang drapes until late that afternoon. Then she walked over to Mrs. Bergstrom's. Putting her face to the screen door, she saw her sitting on the sofa.

"Hi. I was wondering if I could see your piano again. Tommy isn't with me."

"Annie, come in. The door is open. I was just writing a letter."

Annie walked in and sat down on the piano bench. "Could I play some keys?"

"Of course. You're really interested in the piano, aren't you?"

She nodded. "My Uncle Johnny was going to teach me how to play, but we don't live near him anymore. He doesn't need to use a music book. He figures out how to play songs by himself. He makes up his own songs, too."

"He's a real musician, then. Maybe you take after him."

Annie shrugged. Secretly, she did believe she took after Uncle Johnny, but it seemed silly to say so when she couldn't play even one song for Mrs. Bergstrom.

"I listen to you play every night while I'm skating, or sometimes I just sit on our porch and listen."

"Why, Annie, that's very nice to hear. I didn't know anyone paid attention."

"Oh, yes, I love to hear you play."

Annie wanted to say something else, something about listening to music after a confusing day with your things lost and the pipes thumping every time you turned on the hot water—how the music made those things go away. She tried to think of how to say what she meant.

The phone rang. "Excuse me, Annie."

Mrs. Bergstrom went to the phone table in the dining room.

"Hello, Steven. I was going to phone you . . . No, I haven't made up my mind yet. I've thought about everything you've said, but it's a big decision . . . Hold a minute, Steven. I have a guest." She put down the receiver and walked to the piano. "It's my son on the phone. I'm sorry, Annie. I'll have to say goodbye."

As she held the screen door for Annie, she said, "I'm so happy we're neighbors!"

Annie walked home, thinking about her song. Where had the notes gone? Everything here was so mixed up. If she could have one quiet day, she was sure the music would come back to her.

The sky was overcast when Annie went out to skate that evening. She heard a few rumbles of distant thunder, and the clouds made the dark come early.

She was sitting on the step, pulling off her skates, when the streetlights flickered and went out. She looked up and down the block. The houses had all gone dark.

She picked up her skates and ran inside. "Mom! There's no lights!"

"I know," her mother called from upstairs. "I've got Tommy here in the tub. Bring the flashlight, will you?"

With Annie to hold the flashlight, Tommy was dried and diapered and put into his crib. Then she and her mother went to the kitchen and set up candles. Annie loved candlelight.

She reached for the handle on the freezer, ready to start their Sunday night dish of butterscotch ripple ice cream.

"Wait. Don't open that," her mother said. "We don't know how long before the electricity comes back on. We can't let the cold air out."

"But it's Sunday."

"I know, but I just spent a small fortune on meat. I can't risk having it thaw."

Up to now, the power failure had been interesting and even fun. But Annie was all set for butterscotch ripple ice cream.

"How about oatmeal cookies?" said her mother. "Oh, drat—they're all gone. How about some raisins?"

That was hardly the same thing, but Annie took a handful and they sat eating them in the soft glow of the candlelight.

"Annie, can we talk about what was bothering you the other day at Cathy's? I know she can be hard to get used to. Is that it?"

That wasn't it. Annie had thought it over. Cathy had made a special effort to be friendly. And Annie had never known anybody who made necklaces and kept a pet shark. She was looking forward to the next visit.

"You're never happy anymore," she said. "Except at her house."

Her mother looked surprised. "At Cathy's? I guess we were going on and on. We must have sounded pretty silly. But I'm happy here, too."

"Not like that."

"Well, not all the time—"

"You're never happy like that at our house," Annie insisted. "You're always working or filling out papers or worrying about something."

"Annie, you have to understand." Her mother's voice began to sound anxious. "So many things need my attention right now. I guess I forgot about them at Cathy's. But if I don't keep track of what needs to be done, we could be in an awful fix."

"You just said you forgot about those things at Cathy's."

Her mother was silent for a minute. "Yes, I did." She watched the candles flicker. "You know, you're right. We can take some time off and everything will be okay. We've been like worker bees. We're overdue for some fun."

She went to the china cabinet.

"I'll bet," she said, setting two glass bowls on the table, "if we open the freezer and shut it again real fast, the meat will be fine. Annie, get the ice cream scoop."

"Yes!"

They ate their butterscotch ripple while the candles burned down to stumps.

"Don't you think an aquarium would be a good thing to have?" said Annie between bites.

"Maybe some goldfish," said her mother. "Let's leave the exotic stuff to Cathy."

Music and Dancing

WHEN SHE CAME down to breakfast the next morning, Annie heard the refrigerator humming.

"The power came back on about midnight," said her mother. "The meat's fine."

They spent the morning rolling out the rugs and arranging the furniture. At lunch, Annie asked if she could go to Mrs. Bergstrom's house.

"I don't see why not," her mother said, scraping up the last spoonful of Tommy's apricots. "I think I may put my feet up and read for a while."

Annie thought that was a wonderful idea. She felt very happy as she cut across the yards. When she went up Mrs. Bergstrom's steps, Annie heard her talking quietly. Maybe she was on the phone. Maybe her son had called. Annie thought of going home, but she looked in the screen door. Mrs. Bergstrom was kneeling on the floor in front of the TV set. The phone was in its cradle.

Mrs. Bergstrom was talking to herself.

"Turn on the power, insert the cassette with the arrow side up, push 'play.' So why doesn't it work?" She sighed heavily.

Annie knocked gently.

Mrs. Bergstrom turned around in surprise. "Oh, Annie, come in," she said, laughing. She seemed embarrassed. "I'm afraid you caught me being an old lady." She struggled to her feet. "Can you show me how to work this thing?"

Annie walked in. She saw that a VCR now sat on top of the TV.

"I think so."

"I feel so idiotic. My son made a special trip to drop it off this morning. He showed me exactly how to play a tape. Now I can't do it. I don't want to call him at his office."

"Well, you need to have the TV on first."

"Oh, I see," Mrs. Bergstrom said. "I didn't understand that. Here, it's on now."

"You have to put on channel four."

"Now I remember, Steven did say something about that."

Annie had a hard time waiting while Mrs. Bergstrom fumbled with her glasses, then carefully moved her finger over every button looking for the right one.

"That one." Annie pointed. "Now switch to 'VCR.' "

Mrs. Bergstrom pushed one button, then another. The TV went off again. "Okay, I pushed 'TV off,' and then 'VCR.' What do I do next?"

Annie thought it was pretty hopeless to try teaching Mrs. Bergstrom about the VCR.

"Oh, dear," said Mrs. Bergstrom, looking at the blank screen, "I guess I didn't do that right. Here, Annie, you'd better take this." She handed her the remote control.

It was different from the one Annie was used to, with more buttons, but she quickly figured it out. The title came on the screen, *Coppélia*, and the name of a ballet company. An orchestra started up. From the first notes, Annie realized that she knew this music.

"Annie, you're a miracle worker. I was fit to be tied. I was so looking forward to hearing this. Can you stay a few minutes?"

Could she. Annie slid into the rocker while Mrs.

Bergstrom settled herself on the sofa. The last of the credits rolled by and the curtain went up on a scene of houses around a village square. An old man came out of the house on the right.

"That's Dr. Coppelius, a sort of inventor who may dabble in magic," Mrs. Bergstrom said. "He makes life-size mechanical dolls. His favorite is the one sitting on the balcony of his house. He calls her Coppelia."

A ballerina came onstage and danced.

"That's Swanilda."

Swanilda seemed to be trying to get the attention of the mechanical doll, who sat holding a book as if she were reading. But Coppelia ignored her, which irritated Swanilda. She stamped her foot. Then she hid when she heard someone coming. A young man appeared.

"That's Franz, her fiancé."

While Swanilda watched, Franz waved and blew a kiss to Coppelia. With jerky moves, the doll—Annie could see it was actually a real person—pulled the book down from her face, blew a kiss to Franz, then sat down again, putting the book back in front of her face. Each move was exactly in time with the music. She was really very funny.

"Can we see that again?" said Annie.

"I think that's the only time she does that."

"No, we can rewind and watch it again right now."

"Can we? Let's do it."

Annie thought everybody knew that you could re-play whatever you wanted on a cassette.

They watched Coppelia blow her kiss three more times. Then they let the tape run. In pantomime, Swanilda and Franz had an argument. Then the people of the village came out and danced to the lively music that the orchestra had played before, the music that Annie knew.

"This is one of the songs you play."

"Good ear, Annie! Yes, this is one of my favorites. It's a mazurka. That's a kind of folk dance."

Mazurka. Annie repeated it to herself. The word was like a door into another world.

Mrs. Bergstrom asked if they could watch that part again. Annie stopped the tape, rewound it, and pressed 'play.'

"Isn't it amazing?" Mrs. Bergstrom said. "We have music and dancing just by pushing a few buttons." She was as happy as a little girl with a wonderful new toy. She tapped her fingers in time to the rhythm and hummed along.

Annie hummed, too, pleased that she knew the melody. It was like being in on a secret.

The mazurka ended, and the music went on.

Annie reached for the remote control. "Should I play that again?"

Mrs. Bergstrom glanced at her watch.

"Oh, dear! Annie, I'm afraid we'll have to hear it again another time. I just remembered, I have an appointment to get my hair cut."

Annie was crushed. This was the nicest afternoon she'd had since they'd moved.

Mrs. Bergstrom got to her feet. "Isn't it too bad that these silly things interfere with what's really important? Annie, will you tell me how to shut this thing off? I really must learn to do it myself."

Annie explained the steps, but she could see how easily Mrs. Bergstrom got mixed up when she tried to follow them. After some confusion, all the lights on the VCR went out. Annie put the cassette in its box and started for the door.

"Wait a minute, Annie." Mrs. Bergstrom sat down at the piano. "I don't need to be in such a hurry. We have a couple of minutes." She lifted her hands to the keyboard and played a ripple of notes, the opening music from the ballet. She took a breath and leaned forward.

She played the mazurka. She played by heart, hardly looking at the keys, as if it were the easiest thing in the world to do. A river of music flowed out of the piano. When the last note had sounded, she put her hands in her lap.

"Thank you for helping me today. I was having an awful time until you stopped by."

All the way home, Annie hummed the melody. Then she sat down on the front steps and played it in her head, again and again.

When she walked into the kitchen, Tommy was sitting in his high chair, finger-painting the tray with chocolate pudding.

"Try to get some of that in your mouth," said Annie's mother, looking over her shoulder. "Hi, Annie. Would you mop up over there? I'm doing these onions."

Annie sighed. How was it possible to make such a mess? Tommy pulled his face away when she tried to wipe it with a damp cloth. "No!" he shouted.

"One other thing. Would you take this bag downstairs and bring me half a dozen potatoes? I put them in a basket in a dark corner so they wouldn't sprout. By the furnace."

About the last thing Annie ever wanted to do was go to the basement again. She set the door open with a shoe to make sure it wouldn't shut behind her.

By now, the sour smell was familiar as she went

down the steps into the half-light. The basket was right where her mother had said. Annie opened her bag and began dropping in potatoes—one, two, three. Her mother's footsteps squeaked in the ceiling above her.

Suddenly, Annie froze. What was that soft scratching, right near her? She held her breath and waited, second after second, in silence. It was nothing. Four, five.

Again, the soft scratching. This time, Annie was sure where it came from—one of the furnace pipes, the one just above her head.

It must be a leaf caught in the pipe. That was it. Or a piece of paper or something. Nothing to be afraid of. The scratching stopped. Then it started again, more insistent this time.

Annie stood absolutely still, listening to the pattern of scratching and silence. This was something alive. She ran back upstairs and threw the bag of potatoes onto the kitchen table.

"There's some kind of animal in our furnace! It's making noises."

"Annie, are you sure? I'm in the middle of dinner here."

"I'm sure."

Annie's mother pulled Tommy out of the high chair and shifted him to her hip. "Let's go."

They went to the furnace. Tommy gurgled and sucked on his fingers.

"Shh, Tommy," whispered Annie.

They waited.

"Annie, I don't—" The scratching started. Annie's mother put her ear to the pipe. "Oh, dear. It sounds like a bird. This pipe leads into the chimney. The bird must have fallen in."

"Why doesn't it just slide down into the furnace? Then, if we open the door, it can get out."

"I'm afraid it's trapped by the damper. That's a round plate like a saucer. It's up here where the noise is coming from. This ring that sticks out of the pipe lets us tip the saucer up or put it down flat. When it's flat, it closes the pipe and nothing can get down into the furnace."

She jiggled the ring delicately. A flurry of scratching started and stopped. "I can see from the ring that the damper is tilted halfway open. The only thing I can think is that the bird is sitting on the damper. Maybe it's caught somehow."

Annie didn't exactly understand everything her mother said, but she understood enough to be angry.

This fat beast had swallowed a bird. She didn't care that it was just a heap of metal pipes.

"We've got to get it out. It'll die in there," she said, feeling that she was about to cry.

Her mother took a step back, frowning intently at the furnace. "I'm trying to think what we can do, Annie." After a minute, she shook her head. "I'm not getting any good ideas."

"We can cut open the pipe."

"No, Annie, we can't. Even if we could, I think the bird would die of fright from the noise. Here, hold Tommy." She gave him to Annie and opened the furnace's square iron door. To Annie's horror, she put her head into the furnace, then struggled back out with soot in her hair.

"I need the flashlight. It's like midnight in there." She hurried upstairs.

As Annie listened to her mother's footsteps above her, she thought of how frightened the bird must be, trapped in the dark. It didn't know where it was. That reminded her of something, but she couldn't think of what.

Her mother came back with the flashlight and a hand mirror. "Maybe I can see what's up there with this." Annie was still trying to catch the picture that was flitting through her head. Something about birds and darkness. Yes.

"Mom, remember the birdhouse at the zoo? Some of it was like a beach and some was like a meadow and there weren't any bars or glass to keep the birds where they were supposed to be? Remember the sign?"

In the birdhouse, the hallways where the people walked were all in darkness. The displays where the birds lived were in brilliant light, like a sunny day. A sign was posted on the wall: WHY DON'T THE BIRDS FLY OUT OF THE HABITAT DISPLAYS? Annie and her mother had read the explanation together.

"The birds won't fly into darkness," Annie said. "They want to stay where the light is."

"You're right. When the bird looks down—"

"All it can see is black. If we make it light in the furnace, maybe the bird will try to get down there."

"We need something white to stuff in there."

Annie's mother took Tommy while Annie ran upstairs. If there was one thing they had plenty of, it was white packing paper. Annie grabbed the smoothest sheets she could find. She was out of breath with excitement when she got back to the basement. This had to work.

They rolled the paper to fit it into the opening,

then flattened it on the furnace grate as best they could.

"Okay, Annie, here goes." Her mother clicked on the flashlight and played the beam over the white paper. No sound came from the pipe. Her mother kept moving the light around. Maybe the bird was really trapped. Maybe it couldn't get out by itself or even see the light.

Suddenly a burst of scratching came from the pipe, much louder than before. Annie knew that the bird was struggling desperately. It must have seen the light. Now it was trying with all its might to get to it.

Annie leaned toward the open furnace door. If only . . .

Bang! A dark shape hit the white paper and shot out of the furnace, just missing her head.

"Annie, look out!"

A sparrow careened toward the shelves. It perched on the skates for a second, then hopped to the tubs. A second later, it was off. *Bang!* It hit the closed window over the workbench and zoomed back toward them again.

Annie yanked a wooden crate up to the workbench, climbed up on it, and reached for the window.

"That's it, Annie!" With her mother helping, Annie lifted the hinged window and held it. The sparrow sat on the top of the furnace studying the open window with a cocked head. It blinked once. It blinked twice. Then it dove past Annie's upraised arms and out to freedom.

"And then tomorrow we can go to the hardware store and get some stuff to fix the birdbath. We can paint it white and put it in the front yard. We can put up a birdhouse, too."

"Okay, Annie, okay," her mother said, laughing, "but now finish your dinner."

Annie looked down at her plate. She'd been talking so much she'd hardly been able to eat. She dug her fork into the mashed potatoes.

"It's really lucky that I went to get the potatoes, or we wouldn't have known the bird was there."

"It certainly was. I'm having someone over to look at the roof on Friday. I'll have him put a guard across the chimney so no more birds can fall in. I'm not sure the birdbath can be fixed, though."

A Song at Twilight

THE NEXT MORNING, Annie and her mother and Tommy went to Mitchell's Hardware and Paints.

The man behind the counter held up a red can.

"Just push this into the crack with a putty knife and let it cure for a day. The birds'll love you."

They loaded the supplies into Tommy's stroller and started down the main street toward home. At the first corner, they waited at a red light.

"Annie?" said a voice behind them. They turned around. Karen stood with Rebecca's leash in one hand and a bag of groceries in the other.

"Oh, hi. Mom, this is Karen. And Rebecca. I told you I met them when I was skating."

"Karen," said Annie's mother, shaking her hand. "It's so nice to meet someone in the neighborhood. I've been too busy to say more than hello to anyone."

The light changed and they all crossed the street.

"I'm going to Amato's Bakery," said Karen. "You've got to taste an Amato's cannoli. It's heaven."

Annie had no idea what a cannoli was, and she wasn't sure she wanted to eat anything from one of these strange places, but Karen was holding a screen door open for them.

As they walked in, Annie could smell good things baking. In the glass cases, rows of rainbow-colored cookies alternated with trays of strawberry tarts and cream puffs. Frosting flowers cascaded over birthday cakes. Pastry horns and sponge-cake shells seemed to explode with whipped cream. Annie saw signs by some of the trays, but she had never heard of "tiramisu," "Neapolitan," or "baba au rhum" before.

"Stay, Rebecca," said Karen, settling her and the grocery bag near the door. Annie was surprised that nobody said anything. In her old neighborhood, dogs were never allowed in stores.

Karen walked up to the counter and put a hand to her forehead. "I'm suffering a cannoli attack, Mrs. Amato," she gasped. "It just came on. I don't think I can take another step."

Mrs. Amato raised her eyebrows.

"Oh, I see, an emergency. You suffered an éclair attack yesterday, I think." She spoke with an accent.

"And these must be two more suffering people." She looked down at Tommy. "And a poor, suffering bambino."

"Yes," said Annie, wanting to be in on the joke. "We almost fainted in the street."

"Not to worry. Mrs. Amato"—she laid a flour-covered hand on her apron front—"can save you. Vanilla or chocolate?"

"Chocolate, please," said Annie. She still didn't know what she was going to get, but by now she was sure it was going to be something wonderful.

Karen asked for the same and Annie's mother ordered vanilla so they could taste both kinds. Mrs. Amato went through a door behind the counter and came back carrying a tray. Annie saw three big crackers on it, rolled into tubes. Mrs. Amato picked up a cloth bag with a nozzle on it and squeezed. Some kind of white frosting flowed into one of the cracker tubes.

Then Mrs. Amato picked up a second cloth bag and squeezed chocolate filling into the other tubes. She handed one to Annie.

"So? Are you saved from fainting?"

Annie took a big bite, expecting sweet chocolate frosting like her mother made. Instead, the filling tasted more like the cheese pie her Aunt Laurie made.

Annie had never really liked Aunt Laurie's cheese pie.

"Uh, it's fine," she said, trying hard to swallow the thick gluey mass in her mouth. She didn't want to hurt Mrs. Amato's feelings.

Mrs. Amato watched her for a moment. "I think maybe you would like something sweeter."

She went out again and came back with still another cloth bag. Annie had just gotten down the last swallow. She couldn't take one more, not even to be polite.

"Now, this," said Mrs. Amato, squeezing the bag over a paper doily that she twirled around, "will save you." She handed Annie a perfect pink rose.

Cautiously, Annie took a nibble. It was pure sugar. It was the best thing she'd ever eaten.

On the way home, Karen told them all about which stores to go to and the delicious things you could get if you knew what to ask for. Annie finished her sugar rose and began licking the doily.

They got to Karen's block.

"See you," she said. Then she and Rebecca trotted across the street, Rebecca's tail waving like a flag.

When they got home, Annie's mother opened the can from the hardware store. Using the spatula they'd bought, she scooped gloppy white stuff out of the can and pushed it into the crack in the birdbath dish.

"I hope this works," she said, as they set the dish in the sun. Annie was sure it would.

After lunch, Annie asked permission to visit Mrs. Bergstrom. She could hardly wait to tell her how they'd rescued the bird and how they were fixing the birdbath. She skipped across the yards and up the steps.

Mrs. Bergstrom was sitting on the sofa with a big book on her lap.

"Annie, come in. I'm glad to see you."

When she walked in, Annie saw that the book was a photo album. She sat down on the sofa and studied it.

Mrs. Bergstrom pointed to the picture of a young woman in a flower print dress with a baby in her arms.

"That's me with my son, Steven. He's grownup now. He's got two children almost your age. And that was our dog, Penny."

"What happened to Penny?"

"She died, many years ago."

"Did she get sick?"

"Oh, no. She died peacefully in her sleep from old age. She was almost fifteen. That's very old for a dog."

"Did you miss her?"

"Yes, I did, Annie. I planted a cherry tree over the place where we buried her in the backyard. It was just a twig. Watching it grow made me feel better. Wait till you see the blossoms on that tree next spring!"

"You mean that great big tree in the back?"

"Yes. I've lived here since I was twenty years old. That's when I got married. This was a new house then. I was so proud of it. And how is your house working out?"

Annie described how they'd rescued the bird from the furnace pipe.

"Annie, how clever of you to have remembered about the birds in the zoo! You have a good head on your shoulders."

Annie shrugged, not sure what to say, but she felt very proud of herself.

Then she told about getting locked in the basement after she'd climbed through the window to save Tommy.

Mrs. Bergstrom's eyes opened wide. "That must have been scary."

Annie nodded. "It was awful. But I don't mind the basement anymore. And now we're fixing the birdbath that was broken."

"Oh, yes, you must have a birdbath," said Mrs. Bergstrom. "It's essential!"

At that moment, Annie would have given anything to be able to play her song for Mrs. Bergstrom.
That would make the afternoon perfect.

As if she read Annie's mind, Mrs. Bergstrom said,
"Aren't you going to play my piano today?"

Maybe, if she tried again, maybe it would come
back.

"Tomorrow. I might have something to play tomorrow."

"Hmm," said Mrs. Bergstrom, "this is quite myste-
rious."

She closed the photo album. Annie thought that,
for a moment, she looked sad. Then she smiled.

"What shall I play later tonight?"

Besides the mazurka, Annie didn't know the
names of the different kinds of music.

"You decide."

"Well, I guess I'll see how the mood strikes me."

Annie had been hoping that they would play the
rest of the ballet this afternoon. Now she had the
feeling that this wasn't a good time to ask. Mrs. Bergstrom seemed to have something else on her mind.

"I hope you aren't tiring Mrs. Bergstrom with
too many visits," Annie's mother said at supper that
evening.

"She says she's glad to see me."

For a moment, her mother didn't say anything. She spooned up more carrots for Tommy.

"Annie, I think I should tell you, Mrs. Bergstrom may be moving. I saw Mrs. Bradley from the real estate office looking over the house after you got back this afternoon. I'm sorry. I know how much you enjoy the music."

Annie could hardly eat after that.

Mrs. Bergstrom didn't play any lively dance tunes that evening. The music that came through the screen door was sweet and sad. Mrs. Bergstrom had looked sad when she'd closed the photo album. Now Annie understood why. She was going to leave her old home. Worst of all, she was going to leave Annie.

Duet

THE NEXT MORNING, Annie gulped down a few spoonfuls of cereal and excused herself from the table. As she ran up Mrs. Bergstrom's steps, she saw that the inside front door was shut. She rang the bell, but she could tell that nobody was home. What if Mrs. Bergstrom had already gone? What if somebody else was coming to pack up her furniture?

Annie sat down on the top step and waited, but nobody came up the walk. Finally, she went home.

Her job that morning was to weed the flower beds and turn the dirt over. She didn't feel like doing it, she didn't feel like doing anything, but it would pass the time. She found the digger on the back porch, along with a pad to kneel on. She threw down the pad at one end of a flower bed and started to work.

The digger made a pleasant *chuck* as it broke into the soil crust—*chuck, chuck, chuck.* Annie turned up clods of soft moist earth and wiggling worms. She covered the worms with handfuls of dirt so they wouldn't dry out. They would help the plants grow. She yanked the pad to a new spot. *Chuck, chuck, chuck.* The scraggly plot began to look like a garden.

Annie pulled the pad around the corner and started to dig the front flower bed. She heard footsteps. Mrs. Bergstrom was coming up the block pulling a cart full of groceries.

"Hello, Annie," she called. "What a good job you're doing on the garden!"

Annie waved. She slapped the dirt off her hands and stood up. One foot had gone to sleep. She shook it hard. Before she could run over, a car pulled up in front of Mrs. Bergstrom's house. A man got out and rushed to take the groceries.

"Mother, if only you'd let me know, I could have picked you up at the market as long as I was coming into town."

"I like the walk, dear. I'm fine with my cart." She stretched up and kissed him on the cheek. "Annie," she called again, "this is my son, Steven."

The man smiled and waved. Annie waved back, but she stayed where she was. She didn't feel welcome. She knelt down and picked up the digger. Mrs. Bergstrom and the man went inside.

After a few minutes, they came back out with lawn chairs. Annie could hear part of what they were saying.

". . . would love to have their grandma nearby . . . Nancy could take you shopping . . . a new mall next to . . . this place by yourself anymore . . . what if . . ."

Against his deep voice, Annie heard the soft notes of Mrs. Bergstrom's.

"You're right, Steven . . . I know . . . I've thought about . . . it's so hard to . . ."

Go away, Annie thought. She rammed the digger into the dirt. Go away and leave her alone. She doesn't want to move.

"Annie! Time for lunch."

". . . shoveling all that snow . . ." the man was saying.

Annie picked at her lunch, then waited anxiously through Tommy's nap. Just after three, she heard him cooing in his crib.

She pulled out the piano bench, pushed back the keyboard cover, and stared at the keys. The notes of her favorite song had to be in her head somewhere. They couldn't just disappear.

But each time she began the song, she got stuck at the same place. The left hand forgot what to do.

How did Uncle Johnny do it? How did he match

up the notes he heard in his head with the right keys? Annie pictured his hands on the keyboard, lit by the tall floor lamp. The keys he pressed made a pattern of light and shadow that Annie liked to watch.

Uncle Johnny had said something about that. What was it? Something about watching the pattern; music was a pattern. That was it. She'd been trying so hard to get every single note right that she wasn't thinking of how the notes went together to make a design. In her daydream, didn't she see a design?

Annie pictured her hands on top of Uncle Johnny's, the way she'd first learned to play. She began again.

From this valley they say you are going . . .

The left hand made a pattern, she could see that now.

We shall miss—
We shall miss—

What was the pattern from there? Didn't his left hand go opposite to the right? Yes, that was it.

. . . your bright eyes and sweet smile . . .

Annie played to the end of the song. She played it
again and again. Now she'd always have it.

All the rest of the afternoon, Annie watched for
the car to go away, but it was still in front of the house
at dinnertime. When she looked out the screen door
afterward, Mrs. Bergstrom and her son were standing
by the car. Annie strained to hear what they were saying.

"Oh. I should have asked you to play something
for me, Mother."

Mrs. Bergstrom patted his arm. "That's all right. I
love you dearly, Steven, but you know you've never
had an ear for music." He slid into the driver's seat
and swung the door shut. "Kiss everyone for me!" she
said, waving.

Annie looked at the clock. It was just past seven-
thirty. What kind of music would Mrs. Bergstrom
play now? Happy or sad? The minutes went by in silence. By eight o'clock, Mrs. Bergstrom hadn't played
at all.

Annie called upstairs to the bathroom where
Tommy was hitting the water with his plastic duck.

"I'm going over to Mrs. Bergstrom's house. Just
for a minute."

"Okay," her mother called down. "Not past eight-thirty."

When Annie peered through Mrs. Bergstrom's screen door, she couldn't see anything at first. No lights were on. When her eyes got used to the dark, she saw Mrs. Bergstrom sitting on the sofa.

"You aren't playing tonight."

"Come in, Annie. No, I'm afraid I don't feel like it."

Annie sat down on the sofa. "Is that because you have to move?"

"I guess you heard us talking. Well, everybody wants me to."

"I don't want you to go."

"Annie, how sweet of you to say that."

"I mean it. I won't be able to hear you play anymore."

"Music means a lot to you, doesn't it? That reminds me . . ."

"Of what?"

"Of myself at your age. That's when I started my lessons."

In the dim light, Annie could hardly see Mrs. Bergstrom's face, but her voice was low and tired.

Annie got up from the sofa and sat down at the

piano. Even in the twilight, the black and white keys stood out clearly. She thought for a moment. Gently, she pressed the first keys down. When the right notes came out, she pressed a little harder. The song began to flow, just the way it had before.

Mrs. Bergstrom leaned forward. "Annie! I know that song. Sing it for me, will you?"

Annie had never sung in front of a grownup before, except with her class at school. Her voice came out hoarse at first.

"From this valley they say you are going . . ."

She played a few wrong notes. Mrs. Bergstrom hummed until she picked up the melody again.

"We shall miss your bright eyes and sweet smile . . ."

Mrs. Bergstrom's voice joined in, a step behind hers.

"For they say you are taking the sunshine
That brightened our pathways awhile."

"Start again, Annie. Now I've got the words." She came over and sat down beside her.

Annie played while they sang the first verse. Then she sang the second verse by herself. Mrs. Bergstrom listened carefully.

> *"Come and sit by my side if you love me,*
> *Do not hasten to bid me adieu,*
> *Just remember the Red River Valley,*
> *And the cowboy who loves you so true."*

"That was beautiful," said Mrs. Bergstrom. "Just play the music now."

Annie played the song through once more. Then she put her hands in her lap. Mrs. Bergstrom sat quietly. Annie wondered what she was thinking.

"Annie," she said finally, "you are a musician. If you don't have lessons, it's a terrible shame. And not with just anybody." She got up and sat down on the sofa. Several more minutes went by. At last Mrs. Bergstrom shook her head. "No, I'm not ready to move. Not yet."

She looked at Annie. "If I stay, would your mother agree to piano lessons for you? Once a week?"

"I'll ask her!" Annie shouted, running out the door.

She took the front steps of her house two at a time. Her mother was in the living room, setting photographs on top of the bookshelves.

"Mrs. Bergstrom is going to give me piano lessons!" Her mother looked around in surprise. "If you say it's okay."

Her mother put up a few more photographs. Annie wondered why she didn't say anything. After a minute, she turned around.

"I'd love to have you take piano lessons, Annie, but I don't know how we'd pay for them. I can barely afford everything we need right now."

"Maybe we could pay her later, when we have some money."

"I don't know when that will be, Annie. I can't ask Mrs. Bergstrom to give you lessons for free. It wouldn't be right."

"But it wouldn't be for free if we paid her later on. Please. You won't have to buy me clothes this winter, since we got all that stuff from Aunt Sharon."

Her mother sat down on the footstool. "Let me think for a minute, Annie. Maybe there's something we can do."

Someone tapped on the screen door. When Annie turned around, Mrs. Bergstrom was standing there.

"Yoo-hoo, may I come in?"

Annie's mother jumped up and opened the door.

"Hello. I'm Margaret Bergstrom from down the block. I guess you know why I'm here."

"I'm Jane Howard. Please sit down. We were just talking about it. Mrs. Bergstrom, I guess I'd better tell you straight out, I don't know how I'd pay for lessons. It took everything I have to get this house."

"Yes, I thought that might be a problem. But I have an idea." She sat down on the chair Annie's mother pulled forward. "I saw Annie fixing up your garden this morning. I'm afraid mine is turning into a weed patch. I can't stay on my knees too long anymore. I thought Annie and I might make a trade. Weeding for piano lessons."

Annie's mother turned to her. "Annie? What do you say?"

"Yes! Yes, yes, yes!"

Her mother looked back to Mrs. Bergstrom. "What about this winter?"

"I'm sure we'll think of something. As you may know, I was thinking of selling my home. It really is too much to take care of by myself. But I believe I could manage a while longer if I arranged for help with the house and the yard." She stood up. "I'm so happy this is settled. Before I go, I want to say what a beautiful job you've done here. It's a real home."

Annie looked around. The boxes were almost gone. Their comfy old furniture was all in place.

"Thanks. I couldn't have done it without Annie."

They decided on Saturday afternoons for the lessons. When the day arrived, Annie could hardly eat lunch.

To pass the time until her lesson, she rearranged her horses, including Red River. The day before, Annie's mother had answered the doorbell to find a package delivery man holding the box with the double-star brand.

Annie kept looking at the clock. At five minutes to two, she went downstairs. Her mother waved from the kitchen as Annie went out the front door.

Three sparrows flew out of the birdbath that now sat—thanks to some help from Karen—in their front yard. As she cut across the lawn, Annie wondered if the sparrow she had rescued was one of them.

She knocked on Mrs. Bergstrom's door.

"Come in!"

Annie opened the door and stared in amazement. Mrs. Bergstrom's polished living room looked the way Annie's had the week before. Boxes flapped open everywhere. Music books covered the velvet sofa, the coffee table, even the table in the dining room. Vases had been pushed aside to make room.

Sitting in the middle of the clutter was Mrs. Bergstrom, wearing an apron, with a kerchief around her head. Her hands were dirty.

"I'd forgotten how much I had in the attic. Isn't this wonderful? And there're still more boxes I haven't brought down yet."

Annie wasn't sure she could even pronounce the words on the music book covers: *Sonatina, Polonaise, Tarantella.*

"I don't think I can learn all this," she said quietly.

Mrs. Bergstrom laughed. "Not all at once you can't. I'm sorry, Annie. I guess I got carried away. Do you want to know the secret? You learn it bit by bit, the way I did."

She went back to the box she was sorting. Suddenly she held up a book with a faded red cover. "Here it is. My first book."

She stood up and set it on the music stand. Annie sat down on the bench. Mrs. Bergstrom was opening the book to the first page when the phone rang. "Excuse me, Annie." She walked to the phone table.

"Hello, Steven."

Annie's stomach twisted. *Go away.*

"No, dear, I'm sorry. My mind is made up . . . I know . . . Steven, I can't talk now. I'm giving a piano lesson. I've found a very promising new pupil. You remember Annie from down the block? I'll call you later. Goodbye, dear."

She walked back to the piano.

"Where were we? Oh, yes. Relax your shoulders. My teacher, Madame Olanska, always said that relaxation is very important. Take a deep breath and let it out. Put your right hand on the keyboard here"—she took Annie's hand—"letting the fingers curve naturally. Excellent."

And so they began the first lesson.